our
generation.

This is Martha & Keisha's story.

MARTHA™ & KEISHA™

CALLING 9-1-1!

BY

SUSAN HUGHES

ILLUSTRATED BY GÉRALDINE CHARETTE

An Our Generation® *book*

MAISON BATTAT INC. *Publisher*

Read all the adventures in the
Our Generation® Book Series

Read more about **Our Generation®** books and dolls online:
ourgeneration.com

CONTENTS

EXTRA! EXTRA! READ ALL ABOUT IT!
Big words, wacky words, powerful words, funny words...
what do they all mean? They are marked with this symbol *.
Look them up in the Glossary at the end of this book.

Chapter One

DON'T GET UP, KEISHA!

I skated hard down the ice toward the net. We were in the final minutes of our hockey game. My team, the Wildcats, had to win. We just had to!

I have the "C" for Captain on my jersey, and I was trying my hardest—but hockey is a team sport. *All* of us have to try hard and work together to win. We'd done that all season. Now, we were playing against a really good team, the Whirlwinds. The game was tied. If we scored one more goal, we would win it—and our AA* team would be in the season championships!

As I approached the net, I looked to my left. Good. Lauren was there, also skating hard.

Candace had the puck. She was zooming down the boards on our right.

Everyone knows Candace is one of the league's top scorers. She has great aim and can lift the puck*.

Two of the Whirlwinds players were hurrying to get into position to block the shot from Candace. The goalie was crouching, her eyes locked on Candace, ready for her.

The time clock was ticking down. Ten seconds, nine, eight…

Candace was skating straight as an arrow. She lifted her stick to shoot…

But suddenly, before Candace took the shot, one of the Whirlwinds players raced into perfect position near the net to block it.

Oh no! Seven seconds, six, five…

Without hesitating, Candace flicked the puck over to me and it landed perfectly on my stick. I reacted instantly. I lifted the stick back and came forward—hard.

Wham! The puck flew across the ice toward the goal. Before the surprised Whirlwinds goalie knew what was happening or where to look, the puck was in the net.

I scored! I scored! The buzzer sounded. The crowd cheered. *The Wildcats won!*

Screaming with excitement, Candace, Lauren, and our two defensive players who had been moving up the ice

behind us, rushed over to hug me. Then all of our players poured off the bench and onto the ice to join us. As a group, we skated over to congratulate Jill, our totally amazing goalie.

"We did it!" we all cried. "We made it into the championships!"

We quickly formed a line and shook hands with the other team, the way we do at the end of every game. Then our team headed back into the locker room to get changed out of our hockey gear, still chattering excitedly.

I took off my gloves, helmet, and neck guard, and then peeled off my Wildcats jersey. Underneath I wore my favorite red T-shirt. I always felt lucky when I wore it, and today, it had worked its magic!

If only Mom and Dad had been here to see my goal! I thought. But Mom had to work late tonight. And Dad was carpooling my little brother, Teddy, and Teddy's friends, to their swimming lesson.

But that was OK. My teammates and I often carpool to the North Humber Arena* because we practice and play so much that none of our parents can be at every single game. Mrs. Florna, Lauren's mom, had brought me tonight.

"Great goal!" Tori called to me as she unlaced her skates. "You won the game for us, Keisha!"

"Thanks, but we won it with our great teamwork," I said. "And Candace's brilliant pass to me. That clinched it, right, Candy?"

She was sitting beside me, and I nudged her, but she didn't say anything.

I think I know why. She and I had both really wanted our coach to pick us as captain this year. So when Coach chose me, I'm sure Candy was disappointed. Maybe even a bit jealous. If Candy had been chosen instead of me, I would have felt that way.

"Ready to go, Keisha? Candy?" Lauren called, as she stood up and slung her hockey bag over her shoulder.

"Yes!" Candy said. She was getting a ride with Lauren's mom, too. She jumped up, and she and Lauren headed out of the locker room.

"Hang on!" I called, tying up my boots. I quickly grabbed my jacket, bag, and stick and hurried out the door after them. "Hey, wait up!" I shouted.

"Fast on ice, slow on land!" Lauren called over her shoulder, teasingly. She and Candy giggled and went through the arena doors and into the main entranceway. I jogged a little to catch up, but I had to weave my way through a crowd of players and parents. I saw the two girls exit the main doors to the parking lot, talking intently to each other, as if they'd forgotten all about me.

I was a bit annoyed. I couldn't remember where the car was parked. So I sprinted through the main doors, and when I saw the girls heading down the sidewalk, I ran after them—full out. "Hey, Lauren! Candy!" I shouted.

And then it happened. I must have stepped on some ice. My feet went right up and out from under me, and I began falling backwards. I managed to put one arm back to break my fall, but as a result, I smacked myself on the forehead with my hockey stick.

I ended up sitting down hard on the pavement. Tears sprang to my eyes. My forehead hurt! My arm hurt even more!

Lauren and Candy were there right away, kneeling beside me.

"Oh, Keisha! Are you OK?" Lauren asked.

"I'm so sorry we teased you," Candy said.

"Yeah, I'm OK," I said, although I really wasn't. I

tried to sit up, but pain shot through my arm.

"Don't get up, Keisha! Your head is bleeding," Candy said, her voice a bit wobbly.

"Just stay put there for a moment," said one of the arena workers, who had hurried over. "I'm calling 9-1-1 for an ambulance," she went on. "Is there a mom or dad with you, girls?"

Lauren's mom came rushing up as I heard the woman speaking to the emergency operator.

"I don't need an ambulance!" I protested, even though my forehead and arm both hurt.

"You'll be OK, Keisha," said Mrs. Florna. "But your head is bleeding a little, so I think it's a good idea to get some professional help."

She helped me to sit up, and then she pulled out her phone. "I'll give your parents a quick call," she said.

"Is your arm OK? Does it still hurt?" Candy asked.

My arm right above my wrist was hurting even more now, so I cradled it on my lap. And I tried to smile, but I couldn't. I didn't really need to go to the hospital, did I?

Chapter Two

COME ON, MARTHA!

I looked up from my book and glanced down at the hockey rink.

I was sitting in my favorite spot, up on a ledge against the rear wall of the Southdale Arena. I like it here because it's quiet. I can do my homework and then read while Mom sits in the stands with the other hockey parents.

My older brother's hockey game had just finished and his team was heading off to the locker room, but I still had a few more minutes. Maybe I could finish this chapter and find out if the main character makes it onto her favorite hockey team!

But after a few sentences, my mind started wandering to, of course, my own team's chance of getting into the upcoming hockey championships*. I play other sports at school, including volleyball and soccer, and I love my dance lessons, too. But I like hockey best!

I started learning when I was five, and I've been playing competitive hockey for two years, since I was seven. I play defense on my team, the Embers, and we've done really well. Our next playoff game would be in two days and if we win that game, we'll be in the championships for sure.

I sighed. I don't mind going to some of my brother's games, but I feel like I go to *all* of them. I can't stay home alone yet, and usually either Mom or Dad is working if the other one is home. So whenever Pete has a game, I have to tag along. And whenever Mom and Dad are home together, they usually both want to go and watch him play, so I end up going, too.

Anyway, Pete's 17, so of course he can stay home alone, but I just wish…I wish Pete wanted to watch *me* play, but it feels like he hardly ever comes.

I understand it, sort of, but still, it feels like Pete and our parents *all* think his games are more important than mine.

"Martha! Mom!" Pete called.

I looked down toward the locker room door. He

was changed and ready to go, with his hockey bag over his shoulder.

"Come on, Martha!" Pete shouted again.

OK, OK, I thought. I slammed my book shut and grabbed my backpack. Usually, I climb down onto the seats and then to the floor because this ledge is kind of high, and I'm not dumb enough to jump, but today—

"Martha, come *on!*" Pete shouted again.

I was so fed up with Pete and all the attention he gets that I did it. I jumped right down off the ledge, right onto the cement floor and—

Ouch! Ouch!

Tears sprang to my eyes, and I quickly sat down on the floor. I'd landed funny on my foot, and it really, really hurt!

Mom was beside me in moments. "Oh, Martha," she said, worried. "Can you get up? No, better not to get up."

I tried not to cry, and then Pete and one of his hockey buddies were there, too.

"Here, honey, let's take your boot off and have a look," said Mom, untying my laces.

But it really hurt when she slipped my boot off, and then my sock. My foot looked all puffy. I bit my lip.

"Pete, could you please call an ambulance?" Mom said in her calm voice. "I think we need to have this looked at by a doctor."

"No, no, Mom," I protested as Pete pulled out his cell phone. "I don't have to go to the hospital."

"I would feel better if someone looked at your foot as soon as possible," said Mom, calmly. "The ambulance can take us straight there, and the EMTs can keep your leg and ankle from moving around, so you won't be in as much pain."

"What's... what's an EMT?" I asked, trying to swallow my tears.

"Emergency Medical Technician," Mom explained. "EMTs are well-trained in emergencies—and always very kind."

"OK," Pete said, putting his phone away. "They'll be here soon. I told them exactly where we are."

"Excellent," said Mom.

So, the one good thing was that my big brother sat right down on the floor beside me, held my hand, and told

jokes to distract me while we waited.
But, oh—did my foot hurt…!

Chapter Three

HERE COMES THE AMBULANCE

Wow—it was so cool being in an ambulance!

"OK for now?" asked Kaylin, the EMT sitting in the back of the ambulance with me. Lauren's mom was in the front with the driver, Will. Jill's parents had given Lauren and Candace a ride home.

"Yes, thanks," I said. I was lying on a stretcher*, just to keep me comfortable. My head had stopped bleeding, and Kaylin didn't even think it would need stitches. Will had lightly wrapped my arm so it wouldn't move, and it didn't hurt too much right now.

"OK, let's go!" said Kaylin. And off we went.

But I was surprised when Will stopped at the very first red light.

"Why aren't we racing through the intersections?" I asked Kaylin. "Don't ambulances always go at top speed?"

22

"Nope," Kaylin answered, with a grin. "This isn't really an emergency. We'll go there quickly, but we don't need to break any records!"

I was a bit nervous about what would happen when we got to the hospital, but Kaylin chatted with me the whole way. She asked me about hockey and the other sports I like to play, and we arrived before I knew it.

She helped me out of the ambulance and into a wheelchair.

"I can walk," I said, but Kaylin rolled me into the emergency department. She asked Lauren's mom to take a seat in the waiting area, and she parked me in the wheelchair beside her. She went to the reception area to tell the nurse at the desk why I was there.

"You'll have to wait until they examine the people with the more serious problems," she explained when she came back, "but it shouldn't take too long."

I thanked her and Will, and then Mom arrived, looking upset.

"Oh, Keisha!" she cried. She gave me a hug and kiss. "How are you?" She apologized to Lauren's mom for not being at the rink and thanked her for bringing me here.

"Everything is fine," Mrs. Florna reassured her. "Keisha has hurt her arm, and scraped her head, but she'll be looked at soon."

When Mom handed me my stuffed bear, wearing his hockey jersey, I said, "Mom, I'm way too old for Beary!" but I hugged him and almost began to cry.

Then everything became a bit of a blur. Lauren's mom went home. Dad was on his way home from the pool with Teddy, and Mom called him to give him an update. And I was seen by a triage* nurse, who took lots of information about me and about the accident. He gave me a temporary sling* for my arm.

"We'll have one of our patient transporters wheel Keisha to an exam room, and you can go with her," the nurse told my mom.

Soon a nice woman brought Mom and me through some sliding doors and down a hallway of little rooms with curtains all around them.

"Here's your examination room, Keisha," the woman told me. She opened the curtains. There was a bed on wheels inside, and a chair beside it. "Let me help you onto the bed. Your mom can sit beside you while you rest for a bit. Someone will come to assess you as soon as they can."

I must have been really tired from all the excitement because, next thing I knew, Mom was waking me up and I was being helped into a wheelchair. Another transporter person pushed me down the hallway in the wheelchair, with Mom walking beside me. "Your head is fine but your arm needs to be x-rayed*, Keisha," Mom told me.

Mom couldn't go into the x-ray room with me, but it wasn't scary. The radiology technician* smiled and positioned me on a stretcher with my arm out from my side. She explained that she needed to put a heavy lead apron over my upper body to block it from the x-rays.

Afterward, Mom and I were brought back to the same exam room to wait. I had just finished telling Mom about the game and scoring the winning goal when someone wearing a white coat came through the curtains.

"Hi, Keisha," she said, smiling at me. "I'm Dr. Bruce. The x-ray results are back, and it seems you have indeed broken a bone in your arm, between your wrist and your elbow."

I swallowed. *Darn.*

"Because you're nine, we're sending you downtown to the children's hospital. We have a good orthopedics* department here, but the other hospital has lots more experience with children's growing bones," she said. "They'll do a great job fixing you up."

Mom smiled at Dr. Bruce. "Wonderful," she said. "Thank you."

For the next few minutes, Mom tried to decide whether to call a taxi or see if Dad and Teddy would come and drive us downtown. Then a nurse came in to discharge* me and mentioned that another patient was being taken by ambulance to the same children's hospital. She had arranged for Mom and me to go with her.

I was helped back into the wheelchair, and then Mom and I were taken to meet up with the ambulance—again.

Chapter Four

X-RAY RESULTS

"So, Dad will meet us at the hospital," Mom told me.

Two EMTs, Kaylin and Will, had arrived in an ambulance and had come inside to find me. They lifted me into a wheelchair, brought me outside, and then helped me into the ambulance. My foot was still hurting, but it felt a lot better now that I was lying down on a stretcher and my leg was supported.

Mom and Pete stood at the rear of the ambulance.

"Are you sure you don't mind taking my car home on your own?" Mom asked Pete for about the hundredth time.

But my big brother grinned from ear to ear. He has his driver's license but doesn't get much chance to drive.

"I'm sure," he told her, so Mom handed him the car keys.

When he turned back to me, Pete looked more serious. "Good luck at the hospital, sis," he said.

Kaylin told us that she would drive the ambulance and Will would ride with my mom and me, in the back.

"Ready to go?" asked Will.

Will helped Mom in and then he followed with his equipment bag.

My foot just couldn't be broken. My mind was spinning.

I needed that foot. I needed it for walking to school, gym class, dance lessons, and, most of all, hockey!

"We'll be there soon," Will said, breaking into my thoughts.

I nodded. *And my foot will be all fixed up soon.*

"So, you were here watching your brother play hockey?" Will asked.

"Yes." I didn't really feel like talking.

"Have you ever thought about playing hockey?" he asked. "We just went to another arena to pick up a girl, a hockey player, who had hurt herself."

"Really?" I asked, interested in spite of myself. "I play, too."

"Oh, so you *do* play!" Will said.

"Yes, and I love it, too," I said. "I play on a AA team called the 'Embers.'"

Will and I talked more about hockey, and before I knew it, we were at the hospital. In a few minutes I was out of the ambulance and in another wheelchair, and Dad was there, waiting.

He gave me a kiss and handed me my stuffed hockey bear, Slapshot. I gave her a little kiss, and I gave Dad one, too.

Will pushed my wheelchair into the emergency room and asked Mom and Dad to sit with me while he went to register me. When Will came back to say goodbye, I thanked him. He had done a really good job distracting me!

ॐ ॐ

Two bones broken. Two. That's what the x-rays showed.

"We're going to send you downtown to the children's hospital by ambulance," the doctor explained. "You're nine, and the doctors at the children's hospital

specialize in looking after children's bones. They'll set the two broken bones in your foot for you, and put a cast on."

When we got down to the emergency room and I was wheeled out to the front door, the ambulance was already waiting. And so were the two EMTs who had brought me here, Will and Kaylin!

"Hey, Martha," said Will, giving me a fist bump*. "We meet again!"

Mom said she'd come with me in the ambulance, so Dad gave me a quick kiss, said he'd take the car and meet us downtown, and hurried away.

But just as Will and Kaylin were about to help me from the wheelchair into the ambulance, a nurse called, "Kaylin! Will!" She was with a girl who was being pushed in a wheelchair. The girl's arm was in a sling. A woman was hurrying beside them. "This is Keisha, and you will be taking her and her mother downtown as well."

"No problem," Kaylin said, brightly. "We know Keisha. We're the EMTs who brought her here this evening! And we have enough room for everyone."

Chapter Five

SIRENS AND FLASHING LIGHTS

"Will," said Kaylin, "what about giving Martha and Keisha a treat for being so brave?"

"Ha! I think I know what you're suggesting!" Will laughed, as he pulled away from the emergency entrance and into the larger hospital parking lot.

Mom and Martha's mom, who were sitting beside each other, looked at Kaylin with interest. Martha and I glanced at each other. What were the EMTs talking about?

Suddenly—*E-EEEEEEEEE! E-EEEEEEEEE!*

The siren! Will had turned it on!

And then he turned on the red emergency lights, too.

Martha and I burst out laughing as they blinked and flashed.

"Woo-hoo!" I whooped.

All too soon, Will was pulling out of the parking lot

and onto the main street and had to turn them both off.

"Thanks, that was great!" Martha said.

"That was so cool!" I cried.

"We're really not supposed to," Kaylin said, with a wink.

I liked Kaylin. She made me feel really special.

My mom and Martha's mom had started chatting, so we had all of Kaylin's attention. *Excellent!* "I know you're an EMT," I said to her, "but what exactly is that?"

"Yeah, is it the same as being a doctor? Or a nurse?" Martha asked. "What do you do?"

"Well, basically, we EMTs respond to all 9-1-1 emergency calls," Kaylin explained. "We help people with all kinds of medical problems, from sprained ankles to life-threatening issues—for example, if someone is bleeding lots or has had a heart attack. Just last night, we helped a man who had an asthma attack* and we helped a woman whose heart stopped."

"Wow!" I said. I was so impressed.

"If we decide someone needs to go to the hospital, we keep her stable until we can get her there. We have lots of medical equipment we can use," Kaylin said.

Kaylin showed us the oxygen cylinder* and a face mask for giving people oxygen.

"And we used this EKG monitor* earlier today to check a patient's heartbeat. We used this defibrillator* to help get her heart rate back to normal and then we rushed her to the hospital."

"Is it scary to have to take care of people when it's an emergency?" Martha asked.

"No, not really," said Kaylin. "Will and I are well-trained, so we know what to expect and how to work well as a team in most situations."

"It must make you so happy to be able to help people!" I said.

"It totally does," Kaylin agreed. Then she got a radio call. "Oops, sorry, girls. I have to answer this."

Mom and Martha's mom were still talking, so I turned to Martha. "Hey, I like your stuffed bear," I said softly. She was holding it beside her, sort of out of the way. Just like I was doing with mine.

"I have one, too," I told her, quickly. "His name is Beary. Mom brought him to the hospital for me." I held him up and showed her.

She grinned. "Oh, he's so sweet! My dad brought mine to the hospital for me. Her name is Slapshot, and she's wearing a hockey jersey just like yours." She held her bear up so I could see. "I love hockey," Martha went on. "I was actually watching my brother play hockey when I hurt my foot."

"Really?" I said. "That's such a coincidence*. I hurt myself at the rink, too. But not when I was playing hockey. I ran out of the arena after my game and fell outside."

"You play hockey?" Martha said, her face lighting up. "I play, too. I play lots of sports, but hockey is my favorite."

"Same with me! Hockey's the best, right?" I said. "I play center* on a AA team in the Squirt division of our league. Our team is actually quite good!"

"I play defense but, otherwise, same here—Squirt division and a AA team," she said, as excited as I was. "My team has only one more playoff game, and if we win, we'll be in our league championships."

"The game my team won earlier today—just before I got hurt—actually put my team into the championships in our league!" I said.

"Excellent!" Martha said, smiling.

Martha and I had so much in common. Plus, she seemed so nice. Maybe we could be friends. Could the rotten luck of hurting my arm really end up having a bright side?

But suddenly, I frowned. *Martha and I play at the same level of hockey. In the same division...*

"What's the name of the league you're in?" I asked.

Martha paused. Suddenly she looked worried, too. Was she thinking what I was thinking?

"The Lower Lakes League," she said. "You?"

"Me too," I said, and my heart sank. We were rivals*.

Chapter Six

I *HAVE* TO PLAY!

Keisha's team was in the same league as mine, and in the very same division? Our teams could end up playing against each other in the championships for the division trophy!

Oh no!

Keisha and I stared at each other. I wasn't sure how to feel or what to say, and she seemed to be having the same reaction.

I thought we were becoming friends, but now… maybe we shouldn't even be talking! Because what would happen if we ended up facing each other in a hockey game in a few weeks, on opposing teams? How could we be rivals on ice—and friends off the ice?

Before we had a chance to even begin to sort this out, Kaylin said, "Here we are, girls!" and Will was parking the ambulance in front of the hospital. He jumped out, came around the back, and opened the rear doors.

"I'll be right back," he said, and a few minutes later, he returned with two wheelchairs. Mom and Keisha's mom climbed out. Then Will and Kaylin helped Keisha and me out of the ambulance and settled us into the wheelchairs.

The whole time I was trying not to look at Keisha— even as they wheeled us through the entrance and up to the triage station.

Our doctors from the other hospital had called ahead. "We've been expecting you two," the nurse said to Keisha and me. "We have your x-rays here, and all your paperwork."

She smiled at Kaylin and Will. "We'll get them seen shortly."

Kaylin and Will said goodbye to us, and Keisha and I thanked them.

"Now listen, we liked meeting you both, but we don't want to see either of you again!" Will teased, as he waved goodbye.

Mom and I were in a little room with a bed, a chair,

40

and curtains around it, just like in the other hospital. A nurse was helping me into a hospital gown when my dad peeked through the curtains.

"Found you, Martha!" said Dad. "How are you now, sweetheart?"

"I'm OK, Dad," I said.

But just like at the other hospital, everything seemed to move very slowly and very quickly, all at the same time. My foot was really hurting now, and I was feeling tired from...everything! A doctor came in, introduced herself as Dr. Sanchez, and gave me some pain medicine. Maybe I dozed off, because the next thing I knew, Mom was gently waking me, and Dr. Sanchez was there again.

"Hey, Martha," said the doctor. "I've reviewed your x-rays, and we've decided to put a cast on your foot to ensure the bones heal faster and properly. I think you were already expecting this."

I nodded, sleepily. "Yeah," I said.

"Someone will come and get you soon," she said. "And I'll come around and speak with you and your parents afterwards."

"OK," I said. "So you'll fix my foot and it'll be fine,

right? And I can play hockey if my team makes it into the championships?"

"That would be great if your team got into the championships!" said Dr. Sanchez. "But...when would they be, Martha?"

"In two weeks or so," I said.

"Hmmm..." Dr. Sanchez frowned. "Martha, no. You won't be able to play that soon."

"Wait a minute," I said. I struggled to prop myself up on my elbows. "What do you mean? I *have* to play."

Dr. Sanchez glanced at Mom and Dad. She shook her head. "I'm sorry, Martha. No."

"But...but if my team advances through the championships? I could play in that final game, right?" I asked. "It wouldn't be for about four weeks or so."

Mom leaned in and put her hand on mine, and Dr. Sanchez said, "I'm really sorry, Martha, but your bones will need to heal after we set them. You won't be able to put any weight on your foot for at least three or four weeks. You won't be playing hockey again this season."

Dr. Sanchez left, and I lay back on the bed. My throat felt tight.

Mom didn't say anything. What could she say? She squeezed my hand and looked into my eyes.

Really soon, another nice person came with a wheelchair and helped me into it. Mom said she'd wait there for me to come back.

I was still trying hard not to cry, and then—there was Keisha in a wheelchair, appearing from between the curtains next door!

"Cast?" she asked me, looking miserable.

I nodded. "Yup. You?"

She nodded.

It still felt awkward between us, but as we were wheeled off down the hallway, side by side, it didn't quite feel as bad as before.

Chapter Seven

JUST NOT FAIR

"So, Keisha, we've got you all fixed up for now," said Dr. Forester. "We've set the bone in your arm, and we've put the cast on."

I nodded. I liked Dr. Forester. He didn't seem in a hurry, and he was really careful about explaining things in a way that I could understand.

The turquoise cast went from my elbow down to my wrist and even around my hand a little. I'd had a choice of several colors, but turquoise is my favorite!

"It's just a temporary cast, right?" I asked.

"That's right," said Dr. Forester. "It will protect your arm for now, but after a bone in a limb breaks, there's usually some swelling. So this cast will become a little loose as the swelling in your arm goes down. You'll need to come back in a week or so, and we'll take this cast off and put a new one on. OK?"

"OK," I said. "As long as the new one is off in time for me to play in the hockey championships. They're in about two weeks or so."

I yawned. It had been a long day and I was exhausted. I couldn't wait to go home.

But Dr. Forester and Mom were exchanging a worried look.

Oh-oh.

"Keisha," Dr. Forester said. He paused. "I explained that we'll replace this cast with the new one…"

"Yes," I interrupted, "but the new one *will* be off in time for the championships, right?"

"I'm sorry." Dr. Forester shook his head. "No."

"No?" I said.

Mom moved closer to me and took my hand.

"Even in the new cast, you won't be able to play hockey for two months or so at least," Dr. Forester said. "That bone needs to heal, Keisha."

I looked at Mom. She just shook her head.

I looked back at Dr. Forester. He shook his head, too. "I'm sorry, Keisha."

It wasn't fair. It just was not fair. All the way home in the car, I couldn't stop crying. I was so tired and so upset.

Teddy had been asleep for hours, but Dad greeted us at the door.

"Oh, munchkin," he said. "This has been quite a day for you!"

But I couldn't even smile at him. "I just want to go to bed," I said.

"Sure thing, Keisha. I understand," Dad said.

But did he? Did he know I wasn't going to be playing for my team in the championships? I couldn't bring myself to explain it to him. Not right now.

"Good night, Dad. Mom. I'm going to go to bed," I said.

Mom offered to help me get undressed, but I said no.

It was a struggle to get changed out of my clothes and into my pajamas with the cast on my arm and hand. And it was awkward brushing my teeth. But it felt good to have something to aim my anger at.

Then I suddenly had an idea. My lucky T-shirt!

Maybe it wasn't impossible for me to play in the finals. What if I wore my lucky T-shirt every day between now and then?

I hurried downstairs, through the kitchen, and into the mudroom*, next to our laundry room. That's where we kept my hockey bag. And that's where I found it now. Lauren and Candace must have picked it up and brought it to my house after I went in the ambulance.

Now the bag was empty. It looked like Dad had hung up my equipment for me and put my hockey underclothes in the hamper. So, I rummaged through the hamper, searching for my T-shirt...

But no. My lucky red shirt. It wasn't there.

I crossed my arms.

Right away, I knew. It made sense. Candace had taken my T-shirt. She wanted it for herself.

ﻼ ﻼ

It had been five days since I broke my arm. Dad had offered to drive me to my hockey team's practice two nights ago.

"Your coach and the girls on your team have been

calling to see how you are," Dad had told me. "They might like to see you in person."

But I said no. I didn't tell Dad this, but I couldn't stand the thought of going and just sitting there watching and not playing.

Then, last night, the doorbell rang while I was upstairs in my room. I heard Mom answer.

"Oh, hi, Candace! How are you?" she said. "Teddy, can you run upstairs and get Keisha?"

But there was no way I wanted to talk to Candace. Not after she took my shirt. So I ran to my bed and lay down, closed my eyes, and pretended I was sleeping. I heard my brother whisper my name from the doorway, but he didn't come in.

When Mom came up later, she brought me a big card. One of my teammates had drawn a picture on the front of me scoring a goal. Inside, everyone had signed it. They wrote, "We couldn't have made it to the championships without you, Captain!"

Today, Kallie, a friend from school, invited me to a sleepover with some other friends this weekend, but I told her I had other plans. And it was true. I did. I planned to sit at home and feel sorry for myself.

"Keisha says she won't go to Kallie's sleepover party this weekend." It was Mom talking to Dad in the kitchen. I was just coming downstairs, and I stopped to listen.

"No?" Dad asked. "That's too bad. She'll miss out on some fun. And Kallie and the other girls will be disappointed."

I bit my lip. I hadn't thought about that. About my friends. Just like I hadn't been thinking much about my teammates.

For a moment, I thought of the girl I'd met at the hospital—Martha. She never told me the name of her team. Had the team made it into the championships? Even if it did, like me, she probably wouldn't be able to play. Was she feeling like me? Was she refusing to go and watch her team practice, and ignoring her friends? Was she being unpleasant to her family?

Every day since the accident, to show how sorry he was for me, Teddy had made me a special drawing at school. He had put it under my pillow for me to find before I went to sleep. I hadn't even thanked him yet.

I came into the kitchen, and my parents smiled at me. "Honey," Mom said. "How are you doing?"

"Yes, how are you feeling, munchkin?" asked Dad.

I still felt sorry for myself, but I'd been thinking only about myself and no one else for days—and I had to stop.

I took a deep breath and forced myself to smile. "Thanks, Mom. Thanks, Dad. I'm feeling a bit better," I said. And as soon as I said it, I did actually feel a bit better!

Chapter Eight

FEELING DEFENSIVE

I couldn't play in the hockey championships. I kept trying not to think about it. I really did. But it was almost impossible. Even the very first night I got home from the hospital. It was so late and I was so tired, but when I finally climbed into bed and shut my eyes, all I saw was my team celebrating the big final win—without me.

I didn't sleep well, because it felt so weird having a cast on my foot, and I couldn't get comfortable.

The next morning, Pete came in as soon as I opened my eyes. He hugged me and offered to drive me to school. He said how sorry he was that I got hurt at the arena. And all I could think about was how lucky he was to be able to play hockey when I couldn't.

It was so frustrating trying to get around the first few days. I was a pretty good athlete, and I always thought of myself as very coordinated and fairly strong.

But whoa—I wasn't very good at using crutches! I moved really awkwardly, and my arms were really sore every night.

Pete did take me to school that first morning, but after that, Mom said she'd take me back and forth herself. My friends were great about carrying my backpack and jumping up to get me things in the classroom. But after we ate lunch, they would usually head off to play outside. Sometimes it would be hard for me to join in, and I didn't really feel like just watching.

So instead I'd go to the library, but my mind would go straight to the championship games. I imagined lacing up my skates and warming up on the ice, and hearing the start whistle. I could feel the excitement of the game, my teammates and I working toward making a goal, protecting our net, the great sense of teamwork, the freedom of whizzing down the ice...

Then the school bell would ring, and I'd head back to class, awkwardly making my way down the hall on my crutches.

Two nights after breaking my foot, Mom asked if I wanted to go and watch my team practice, and I said I had too much homework. Even though I didn't.

And the next night, Dad said he'd take me to watch the Embers play in our first championship game. I lied again. I said I wasn't feeling well.

I just couldn't do it. I felt so left out.

The next evening, I ended up going to another one of Pete's games. Both Mom and Dad were home, so one of them could have stayed home with me. But Pete's team was closing in on making the championships in his league and they both wanted to watch him play. They didn't even *ask* me if I wanted to go along.

I didn't say much as we watched. I sat there, trying not to picture my own team playing, and me out there playing defense. Trying not to think about how Mom, Dad, and Pete all thought his league and his games were more important than me and mine.

But I wasn't succeeding. I was getting so angry.

Then I remembered Keisha, the girl I'd met in the ambulance. I bet she'd understand just how I was feeling. She probably couldn't play in the championships either.

I wished I could talk to her, even for a few minutes. Was she finding it hard to stop thinking about what she was missing? About how she'd looked forward to the championships all season long—and now couldn't play?

Somehow, thinking about her made me feel less alone. I felt sorry for her, but it was kind of nice to know she might be feeling exactly like me. Understanding what I was going through. Even though she was on an opposing team.

It made me feel less alone *and* less sorry for myself.

Suddenly there was a big cheer. Pete's team won the game! They'd won! Mom and Dad were yahooing, and yes, that was my brother out there, doing well!

And I got up, broken foot and all, and I cheered, too. I was so happy for him!

Chapter Nine

'C' ON THE JERSEY

"Keisha, you're still captain of your hockey team," Mom said. "Dad and I really think you should go to watch and support your team in their first championship game in the series."

Dad nodded.

I didn't really feel like the captain anymore. And they had probably replaced me with someone else. With Candace. But I said, "OK."

My parents were right. I should support my team.

And the arena has six rinks, and although our team wasn't playing Martha's team tonight, maybe her team was playing another team in another rink. Maybe I'd see Martha. It might feel good to see how she was doing—even if we couldn't be friends because we were rivals.

"Why don't you go in the locker room, munchkin? Give your team a pep talk before the game?" Dad suggested when we arrived.

But I told him, "Not this time."

It was hard being up in there in the stands watching while my team members came out of the locker room and skated onto the ice, so strong and fast. Especially when I saw that Candace had a C on her jersey and was the captain now. But when they all saw me there and waved to me, I made myself wave back.

When the game began and Candace skated up to take the first face-off*, something I used to do, I told myself it was OK. I'd forget about the lucky T-shirt. Candace is a really good player. Everyone looks up to her. She deserves to be captain.

"The Wildcats are playing so well!" Dad said, applauding enthusiastically as Candace scored another goal.

Mom clapped hard, too, but I could only do little careful claps because of my arm.

My team was playing the Wings, a team ranked closely to ours. But we were totally outplaying* them. The score was 2 to 0 for us at the end of the first period. In the third period, we were winning 6 to 2.

Now it was the final few minutes of the game. Lauren took a shot from the blue line* and made a beautiful goal. It was 7 to 2—and the buzzer went off.

Mom and Dad jumped up, cheering, and I jumped up, too. We'd won the game and were moving on in the series and I should be feeling fantastic. But I wasn't. Part of me still felt left out. Jealous even.

I tried to be 100 percent happy for the Wildcats, but I just couldn't do it.

Chapter Ten

BREAKING THE ICE

It was that other girl, Keisha! The one who plays hockey, like me.

Mom and I sat in the crowded waiting room in the orthopedics area of the children's hospital. Why was Keisha here, too?

I waved at her, happily. But then I felt weird. My team had advanced in the championship finals, and maybe her team had, too. In a few days, in only a few more games, we'd know if we'd made it to the final championship game. What if both our teams ended up playing each other?

"Well, hello!" my mom said when she spotted Keisha's mom. "How are you two doing? How's the arm, Keisha?"

Keisha's mom smiled, and she and Keisha came toward us.

"Keisha is here to get her temporary cast off and her

permanent one put on," Keisha's mom explained.

"Same with Martha," Mom said. She looked around but the only free seats were on the other side of the room, so she stood up. "Keisha, why don't you sit here with Martha, and your mom and I can go and sit over there? That way you two girls can have a chat, and your mom and I can, too."

"That would be very nice," Keisha's mom said.

Keisha looked at me and then quickly looked away. "Oh, no, that's OK…"

But Keisha's mom insisted. She and my mom headed together across the room, so Keisha pretty much had to sit down next to me. She didn't say anything for a long time, and I just sat looking down at my leg in its cast, feeling uncomfortable.

Finally, I couldn't stand the silence any longer. "I guess you kind of feel like me," I blurted out.

"What do you mean?" she said.

"Like we can't be friends." I shrugged. "Like we shouldn't even talk. Because we're on opposing hockey teams."

"Yes!" She smiled, a big relieved smile. "Exactly.

You understand!"

"Completely," I said. "Of course."

Now neither of us said anything for a long time. But at least I was smiling, and so was Keisha. And even though we should have felt more awkward maybe, the awkwardness was completely gone.

Keisha said, hesitantly, "I understand how you feel, and I feel the same, but...are we right? We can't be friends?"

"I don't know." I shook my head. "I wish we could. What do you think?"

"I don't know either. I wish we could, too," Keisha said. She bit her lip. "Maybe it's OK to talk a bit? We're sitting right next to each other. It would be rude not to talk, right?"

"So rude!" I agreed.

So we started talking. And whoa, once we began, we couldn't stop. First, I saw the tip of Keisha's stuffed bear's head peeking out of her backpack. "Beary, right?" I said, and Keisha looked a little embarrassed.

But I zipped open my backpack and showed her what was inside.

She laughed. "You brought Slapshot!"

"Naturally," I said.

We compared the bears for a few minutes, and then Keisha asked, "How's it been at school with your broken leg, Martha?"

I told her. I didn't hold back. I did lots of complaining. And Keisha nodded as though she understood. Then she had a turn, and complained about being at school with her broken arm.

I decided to be brave, and I asked her about hockey. Whether she'd been going to watch her team. How that was going.

Keisha didn't reply for a minute. Then everything seemed to just spill out. She told me how hard it was not to be playing. How she didn't even want to go and watch her team play. How another teammate had taken over as captain.

I found myself confiding all kinds of things, too. How I lied so I wouldn't have to watch my team practice. How I'm afraid my parents think Pete's games are more important than mine.

She didn't give me any advice, and I didn't give her

66

any. We didn't criticize each other either. And we didn't say, "Oh, it's not as bad as you think."

We just listened to each other, nodded, and said, "Yes, I know what you mean." It felt really good to have someone understand.

"It's so strange that we met in an ambulance," I said, "instead of at a hockey rink. Remember how amazing the ambulance ride was? Kaylin and Will were so great."

"They sure were," Keisha said, enthusiastically. She paused. "You know, I've just had this idea. Maybe that's something I might want to do one day." Her face lit up. "It would feel good to help other people—and it would be exciting to drive an ambulance!"

"Totally," I said, laughing. "You know, I'm not happy about breaking my foot but it hasn't been all bad spending so much time in the hospital. I've started thinking that I might want to be a doctor one day."

Keisha held up her not-broken hand, and we high-fived.

I was just about to ask her for her phone number, when—"Keisha...?" a technician called. He stood at the front of the room, holding a clipboard.

Keisha jumped up and her mom hurried over.

"That's us!" Keisha's mom called to the technician.

Her mom said to me, "Good luck with your foot and getting your new cast on, Martha!"

Mom said, "You too!" to Keisha.

Then before Keisha and I had a chance to say a proper goodbye, she was gone.

Chapter Eleven

LUCKY T-SHIRT

This was it. My team, the Wildcats, had made it into the final championship game. I could hardly believe it.

Mom, Dad, Teddy, and I were at the rink a little early because I wanted to go and say hi to everyone in the locker room. Yes, ever since I'd talked to Martha that day in the hospital my feelings had changed. I got over feeling angry about breaking my arm and being jealous about not playing hockey, and I was 100 percent excited for my team to do well. To win!

I hurried into the locker room.

"Keisha!" cried Lauren, happily, spotting me first. "It's about time!"

Then everyone was jumping around and greeting me, and asking how I was.

"I'm fine, and thank you all so much for the cards and for checking up on me," I said. "I want you all to play your best, and win this game!"

The girls all laughed and cheered. They sat back down, and continued getting suited up, including Candace.

I hurried over to speak to her, because she was the other reason I'd come early. I was still certain she had my lucky T-shirt, and I wasn't angry about it now. Instead, I wanted to be absolutely sure she was wearing it. If it could help her and the team win, it was fine with me!

But before I got to her, Tori tapped me on the shoulder.

"Hey, Keisha. I'm so sorry, but I've just discovered your T-shirt in my bag. It must have got thrown in there somehow on the day you broke your arm and hurt your head." Tori handed me my red shirt, all wrinkled. "It's been buried at the bottom of my stuff for weeks!"

What? I couldn't believe it.

All this time I had been secretly blaming Candace for taking my shirt! Oh, wow. I was so ashamed, and so relieved that I hadn't accused her.

"Tori had your shirt all this time?" Candace said in surprise when I sat down beside her. "Well, you should wear it in the stands anyway, Keisha. That'll help us win!"

"No way, Candy," I said, shaking my head. "With you as captain, our team doesn't need any extra luck. But *you* can wear my shirt tonight, wrinkles and all—if you want."

"Oh, Keisha. Thank you," Candace said. Her eyes were shining. "I'd love to wear it just this once. But we all miss you. And next year, you'll be team captain again, we'll practice and play just as hard, and you'll be wearing the T-shirt in the championships, OK? Promise?"

I couldn't speak. So I just nodded.

Chapter Twelve

BETTER TOGETHER

Mom and I walked quickly into the arena. I was so glad I didn't need crutches anymore. I had a walking cast* and so I didn't move as slowly as before.

Together, we found the correct rink. We were a bit late, and the game was about to begin—a really important game. The Embers were playing the Wildcats in the championship game.

Was I excited? *Yes!* Ever since Keisha and I had talked in the hospital, I'd decided to forget about comparing the way my parents felt about Pete's hockey games to my games. Plus, all my mixed feelings about my team had vanished.

Now, I was just happy to be here watching them play—and rooting for them to win.

Mom and I got settled and the whistle blew to start the face-off when... "Hey, shove over, sis!"

It was Pete—and Dad was sitting down next to him!

"What are you two doing here?" I asked, surprised.

"It's your championship game, isn't it?" asked Dad. "Of course we'd be here."

"But I'm not even playing," I replied.

"But it's your team, right?" Pete asked. "We want to support you and your team, no matter what!"

I couldn't believe it. I could only grin at them.

At some point during the game, I suddenly thought, *Keisha might be here!* I looked across the arena. That's where family and friends of the opposing team usually sit. Sure enough—there she was!

Amazingly, at that exact same second, she happened to look my way. Without caring one bit about what my family or the supporters of my own team might think, I shot up my hand and waved to her. She waved back.

"Hey, is that Keisha, the girl from the hospital?" Mom asked, peering across the rink. "Are the Wildcats her team?" She smiled. "How wonderful that both your teams made it into the championships!"

"It sure is!" I agreed.

The rest of the game was even more fun to watch now that I knew Keisha was here, too. I was jumping up and cheering for the Embers, and Keisha was doing the same for the Wildcats—and it was perfectly OK.

I was so happy. Keisha and I could be rivals and friends, both at the same time.

It was about eight weeks after the championship, and hockey season had long been over.

I hurried into the hospital.

But not because anything was wrong. In fact, just the opposite.

"Hey, Keisha!" I called. She stood inside, waiting for me.

"Hey, Martha!" Keisha waved with her right hand. Her cast was off, and her arm was fine now.

My cast was off, and my foot was fine, too!

"All set?" Keisha asked.

"Yup. You?" I asked.

Keisha and I had met up quite a few times in the last few weeks, and we'd come up with a plan. We both wanted to learn more about first aid, medicine, hospitals, and ambulances. And we also wanted to help other kids who were hurt or sick.

So here we were—about to begin our first volunteering session at our local children's hospital.

"I'm a bit nervous, but I'm excited," Keisha said.

"Me too," I said. "So look who I brought!" I held up Slapshot.

"Me too!" Keisha said, and she held up her Beary.

We both burst out laughing.

Just then, a nurse came out into the waiting area and smiled. "All the new volunteers beginning today, welcome!" she called. "Please come with me!"

Keisha and I helped Slapshot and Beary exchange a high five—and off we all went, new friends on a new adventure together.

Glossary

Many words have more than one meaning. Here are the definitions of words marked with this symbol * (an asterisk) as they are used in this story.

AA, pronounced "double A": *a high-level of competitive play in youth hockey*

arena: *a building where sports are played in an area surrounded by seats. Example: a hockey arena has an ice rink*

blue line: *one of the two blue lines on the ice that shows players where they can and cannot go*

asthma attack: *when a person with asthma (a lung disease) suddenly has trouble breathing*

center: *a hockey player whose main zone of play is the middle of the ice*

championships: *a series of games to determine the final winner*

coincidence: *when two or more things happen at the same time, in a way that seems surprising*

defibrillator: *an electronic device that gives an electric shock to the heart to help restore the normal heartbeat*

discharge: *allow a patient to leave the hospital*

EKG monitor: *a device that records information during an electrocardiogram (EKG or ECG), which is a test to measure how a heart is working*

face-off: *when the referee drops the puck between two opposing hockey players to begin or to restart the play*

fist bump: *when two people tap each other's clenched fists as a greeting or sign of agreement*

lift the puck: *to hit the hockey puck in a way that lifts it off the ice*

mudroom: *a small room where shoes and jackets can be removed before entering the house*

orthopedics: *the field of medicine that corrects problems with bones or muscles*

outplaying: *playing better than the person or team you are competing against*

oxygen cylinder: *a metal container that stores air needed for breathing*

radiology technician: *a medical person who performs x-rays*

rivals: *players or teams who compete against one another*

sling: *an adjustable bandage that loops around the neck and shoulder to support an injured arm and keep it from moving*

stretcher: *a lightweight, folding bed on wheels used for carrying an injured person in an ambulance*

triage: *the process of deciding which patients need to be seen first in an emergency room*

walking cast: *a cast with a special heel built into it so a patient can walk with the cast on*

x-ray: *a medical procedure using radiation which can go through the body and produce a type of photograph that will show breaks in bones*

On their ambulance rides and in the hospital, Martha and Keisha were helped by EMTs, nurses, and doctors. Later, they also found a way to help kids by volunteering at the children's hospital—and even brought Beary and Slapshot!

these are my ideas for helping other kids:

Martha and Keisha Go to the Hospital

Martha and Keisha learned a lot about ambulances, hospitals—
and each other—when they were injured! A list of hidden words
from their adventure is below. Make a copy of the next page.
Then find and circle the words from the list
that are hidden in the grid.
Here's a hint: the words go up, down, forward, backward
and diagonal (from one corner to the other)!
The solution is on page 84 (at the end of the book).
No peeking yet! ☺

AMBULANCE
BEARY
BROKEN
CAST
CRUTCHES
DEFIBRILLATOR
DOCTOR
EMERGENCY
HOSPITAL
NURSE
SLAPSHOT
SLING
STRETCHER
WHEELCHAIR
X-RAY

Word Search

Q	J	G	E	T	P	H	W	L	H	T	N	U	O	K
F	U	N	W	S	O	Q	I	I	N	Z	N	O	Y	S
Y	M	G	B	H	R	H	Y	H	N	Q	P	O	T	K
D	Z	G	E	O	E	U	S	M	L	P	P	R	U	O
K	T	X	U	G	W	E	N	P	U	P	E	S	Z	L
D	E	F	I	B	R	I	L	L	A	T	O	R	Y	A
S	T	H	N	B	F	A	Y	C	C	L	H	F	A	T
A	Z	O	D	K	R	A	V	H	H	H	S	D	M	I
X	X	L	Z	Q	R	O	E	C	Y	A	N	L	B	P
X	E	A	Q	X	K	R	K	U	B	D	I	X	U	S
C	R	U	T	C	H	E	S	E	B	O	N	R	L	O
Y	C	N	E	G	R	E	M	E	N	C	T	U	A	H
J	N	R	Q	Y	N	R	A	Y	S	T	S	P	N	P
A	B	U	I	D	T	R	S	B	Q	O	A	X	C	A
G	N	I	L	S	Y	A	K	Q	V	R	C	T	E	V

83

Word Search Solution

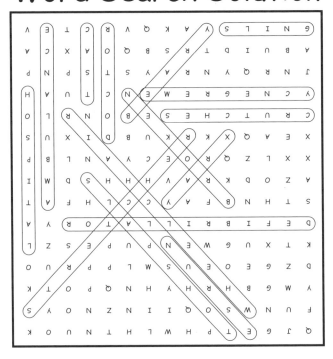

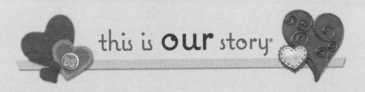

this is **our** *story*

We are an extraordinary generation of girls. And have we got a story to tell.

Our Generation® is unlike any that has come before. We're helping our families learn to recycle, holding bake sales to support charities, and holding penny drives to build homes for orphaned children in Haiti. We're helping our little sisters learn to read and even making sure the new kid at school has a place to sit in the cafeteria.

All that and we still find time to play hopscotch and hockey. To climb trees, do cartwheels all the way down the block and laugh with our friends until milk comes out of our noses. You know, to be kids.

Will we have a big impact on the world? We already have. What's ahead for us? What's ahead for the world? We have no idea. We're too busy grabbing and holding on to the joy that is today.

Our Generation® brings imagination into everyday life, and empowers children to create the narrative of their generation.

Yep. This is our time. This is our story.

ourgeneration.com

About the Author

Susan Hughes is an award-winning author of more than 30 children's books, including picture books, chapter books, young adult novels, nonfiction books for all ages, and even a graphic nonfiction book. Susan is also a freelance editor and writer.

She helps coach and guide other writers in revising and polishing their own manuscripts.

About the Illustrator

Passionate about drawing from an early age, Géraldine Charette decided to pursue her studies in computer multimedia in order to further develop her style and technique. Her favorite themes to explore in her illustrations are fashion and urban life. In her free time, Géraldine loves to paint and travel. She is passionate about horses and loves spending time at the stable. It's where she feels most at peace and gives her time to think and fuel her creativity.

Calling 9-1-1! became the book that you are holding in your hands with the assistance of the talented people at Maison Battat Inc., including Joe Battat, Dany Battat, Loredana Ramacieri, Sandy Jacinto, Laurie Gaudreau-Levesque, Ananda Guarany, Cynthia Lopez, Véronique Casavant, Arlee Stewart, Natalie Cohen, Joanne Burke Casey and Pamela Shrimpton.